MIDNIGHT AT THE MUSEUM

RICHARD & PAMELA WOLFE

SCHOLASTIC
AUCKLAND SYDNEY NEW YORK TORONTO LONDON

FOR DAPHNE

First published by Scholastic New Zealand Ltd, 1997
Private Bag 94407, Greenmount, Auckland, New Zealand.

Scholastic Australia Pty Limited
PO Box 5790, Gosford, NSW 2250, Australia.

Scholastic Inc
555 Broadway, New York, NY 10012-3999, USA.

Scholastic Canada Ltd
123 Newkirk Road, Richmond Hill, Ontario L4C 3G5, Canada.

Scholastic Limited
1-19 New Oxford St, London, WC1A 1NU, England.

Text © Richard Wolfe, 1997
Illustrations © Pamela Wolfe, 1997
ISBN 1 86943 341 6

9 8 7 6 5 4 3 2 1   7 8 9/9 0 1 2 / 0

Edited by Penny Scown
Typeset in 18/24 Garamond Light Condensed
Printed in Hong Kong

Museums are places
full of glass cases
    and animals of all shapes and sizes.
At the end of the day,
when the crowds go away,
    there are more wondrous surprises . . .

The guards lock the doors
and sweep all the floors
    and put on their coats to leave,
but only we know
that after they go
    things happen that they
    wouldn't believe . . .

During the day
the animal display
   all seems so tidy and neat.
But soon after five
it all comes alive
   and runs the place right off its feet!

Animals and birds,
in flocks and in herds,
    climb out of their dusty old cases.
They want to have fun,
to jump and to run,
    play games, sing songs and run races.

8

After standing all day,
they can't wait to play
and party on right through the night.
Monkeys and bears
run up and down stairs —
it's such a remarkable sight.

An emu might squawk
and stop for a talk
  with an antelope, hippo or seal.
Zebras might stroll
with a rhino or mole
  and do whatever they feel.

There's nothing so funny
as a moa and a mummy
　singing a song with a fish!
Skeletons rattle,
and parrots all prattle —
　the animals do as they wish.

14

EGYPTIAN
MUMMY
1300 B.C

A camel might chat
with a large spotted cat,
    and pause for a quick cup of tea.
A lizard might take
    a walk with a snake —
        there are many old friends
            to see.

17

Calling out names
and playing new games,
   the animals go faster and faster.
They can even be found
racing around
   with statues of marble and plaster!

18

The museum is ringing
with laughter and singing.
    Everyone's having a ball!
The lion might pause
to sharpen its claws
    or listen to the brown kiwi call.

21

Out in the park
it's all very dark . . .
    but the museum is lively inside.
An ape on the back
of a large woolly yak
    is having a hair-raising ride!

Suddenly they shout:
Our time has run out!
  Morning has almost begun!
Everyone cries
as the sun starts to rise
  and marks the end of
    their fun.

24

No. 6.
Brown Bear

Common Cassowary

So back up the stairs
go tigers and bears,
  returning to all their old cases.
They don't make a sound,
stop running around,
  and stand in their usual places.

It somehow seems right
that all through the night
  the animals have all this fun,
for during the day
they're all locked away
  unable to frolic and run.

Can you
identify any
of these animals?

No 24

So now when you go
to a museum, you'll know
just what the animals do.
Don't tell anyone
about all their fun . . .
it's a secret, and we've only told you!